Look at a Birch Tree

by Patricia M. Stockland

first step nonfiction

Lerner Publications Company · Minneapolis

root

This is a root of a birch tree.

This is a trunk of a
birch tree.

branch

This is a branch of a birch tree.

This is a leaf of a
birch tree.

seed

This is a seed of a
birch tree.

This is a birch tree!

The images in this book are used with the permission of: © Julie Keen/Shutterstock.com, p. 2; © GAP Photos/Elke Borkowski, p. 3; © GAP Photos/Matt Anker, p. 4; © Stocksnapper/Dreamstime.com, p. 5; © Masslov Dmitry/Shutterstock.com, p. 6; © Lane Erickson/Dreamstime.com, p. 7.
Front cover: © DDCoral/Shutterstock.com.

Lerner Publications Company
A division of Lerner Publishing Group, Inc.
241 First Avenue North
Minneapolis, MN 55401 U.S.A.

Website address: www.lernerbooks.com

Main body text set in ITC Avant Garde Gothic Std 21/25.
Typeface provided by International Typeface Corp.

Library of Congress Cataloging-in-Publication Data

Stockland, Patricia M.
      Look at a birch tree / by Patricia M. Stockland.
         p.   cm. — (First step nonfiction. Look at trees)
      Birch tree
      ISBN 978–1–4677–0524–0 (pbk. : alk. paper)
      1. Birch—Juvenile literature. I. Title. II. Title: Birch tree. III. Series: Stockland, Patricia M.
   First step nonfiction. Look at trees.
   SD397.B5S76   2013
   583'.48—dc23   2012013240

Manufactured in the United States of America
1 – BP – 7/15/12

LERNER

SOURCE

Expand learning beyond the printed book. Download free, complementary educational resources for this book from our website, www.lerneresource.com.